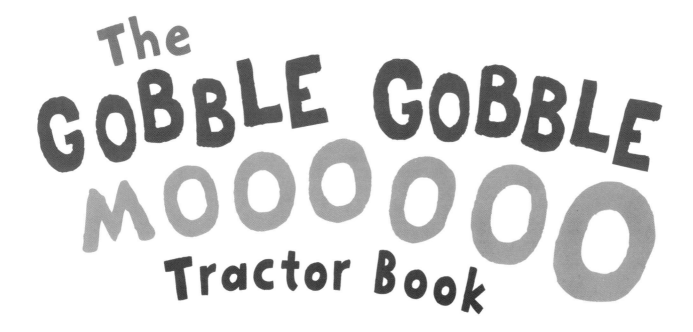

# The GOBBLE GOBBLE MOOOOOO Tractor Book

## Jez Alborough

HarperCollins *Children's Books*

For Sue, from Jez

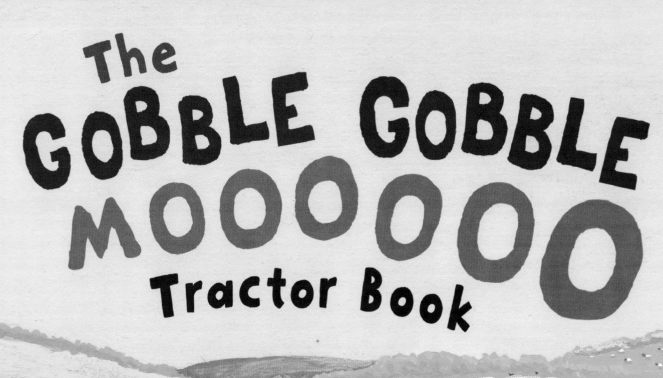

# The GOBBLE GOBBLE MOOOOOO Tractor Book

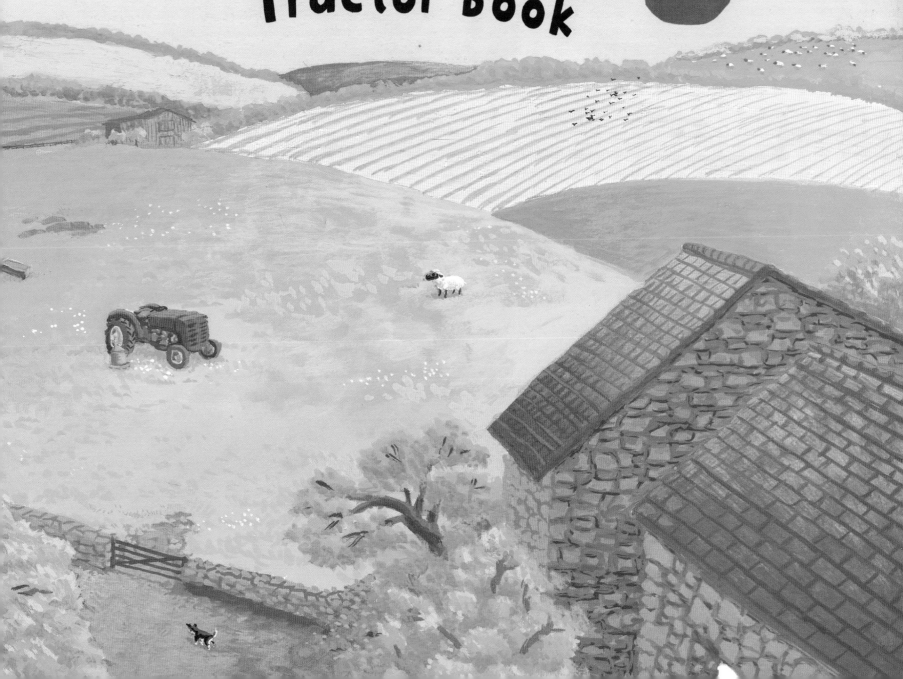

Early one morning,
when Farmer Dougal
was still asleep...

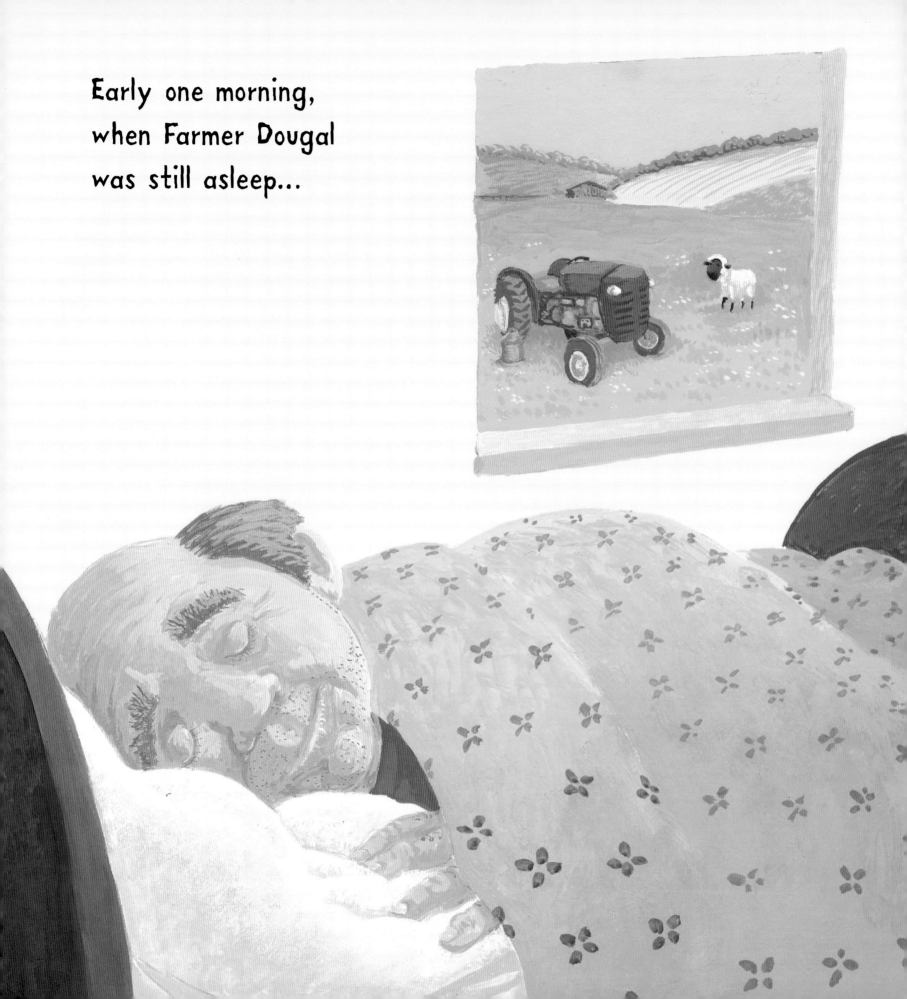

**Sheep** climbed up on to the big red tractor.

'What are you doing?' asked **Cat**.
'I'm going for a ride,' said **Sheep**.
'This is the sound the tractor makes
when you turn the engine on...

'Can I come?' said **Cat**.
'I can do the sound the engine makes
when it starts to wiggle and jiggle...

PURRR

R R

'Wait for me!' said **Turkey**.
'I can do the sound the tractor makes when it drives off down the lane...

GOBBLE
GOBBLE
GOBBLE

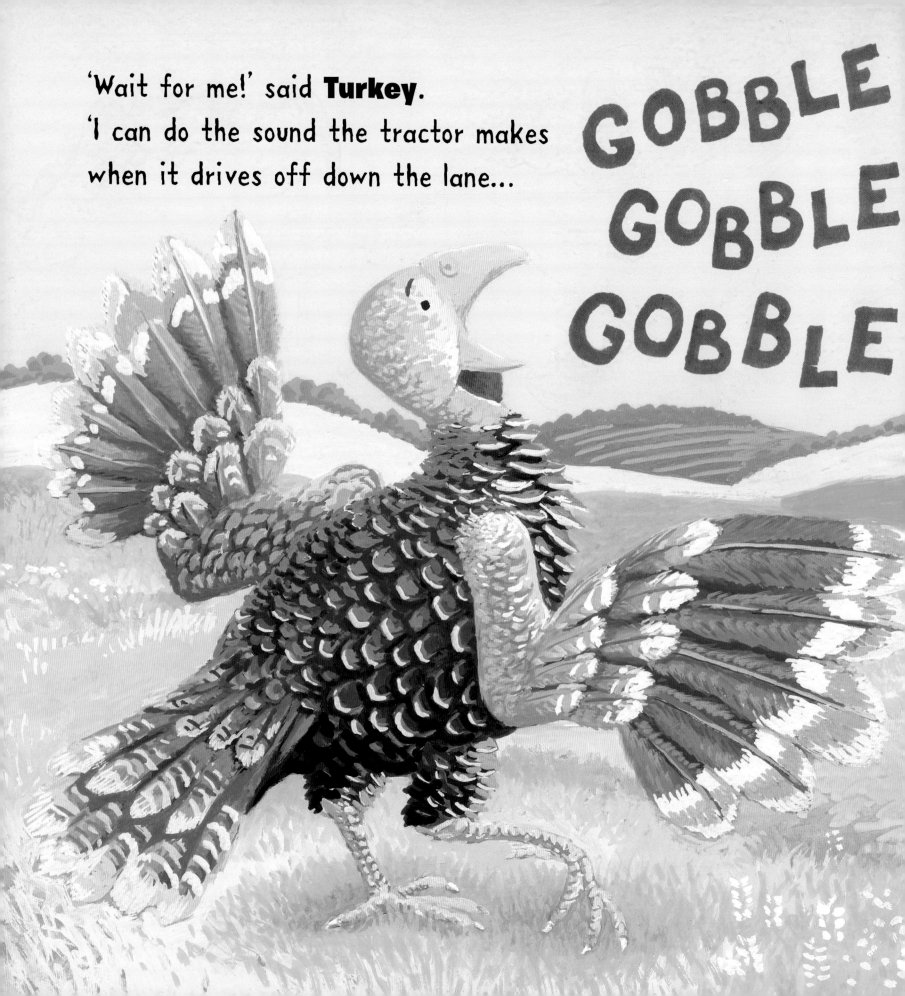

'Let's do it again,' said **Cat**.
'But what about Farmer Dougal?' said **Sheep**.
'What if he wakes up and sees us?'

GOBBLE

Cat and **Turkey** looked at **Sheep**
with two silly smirks and said

P·L·E·A·S·E

'All right,' said **Sheep**.

'Let's go for a ride. READY...

'It's wiggling and jiggling...

PURRRRR

and the tractor is
driving off down the lane...

GOBBLE
GOBBLE
GOBBLE
GOBBLE

'Can I come too?' said Mouse.
'I can do the wheels!
The great big wheels
which go round and round
with a...

SQUEAK SQUEAK
SQUEAK

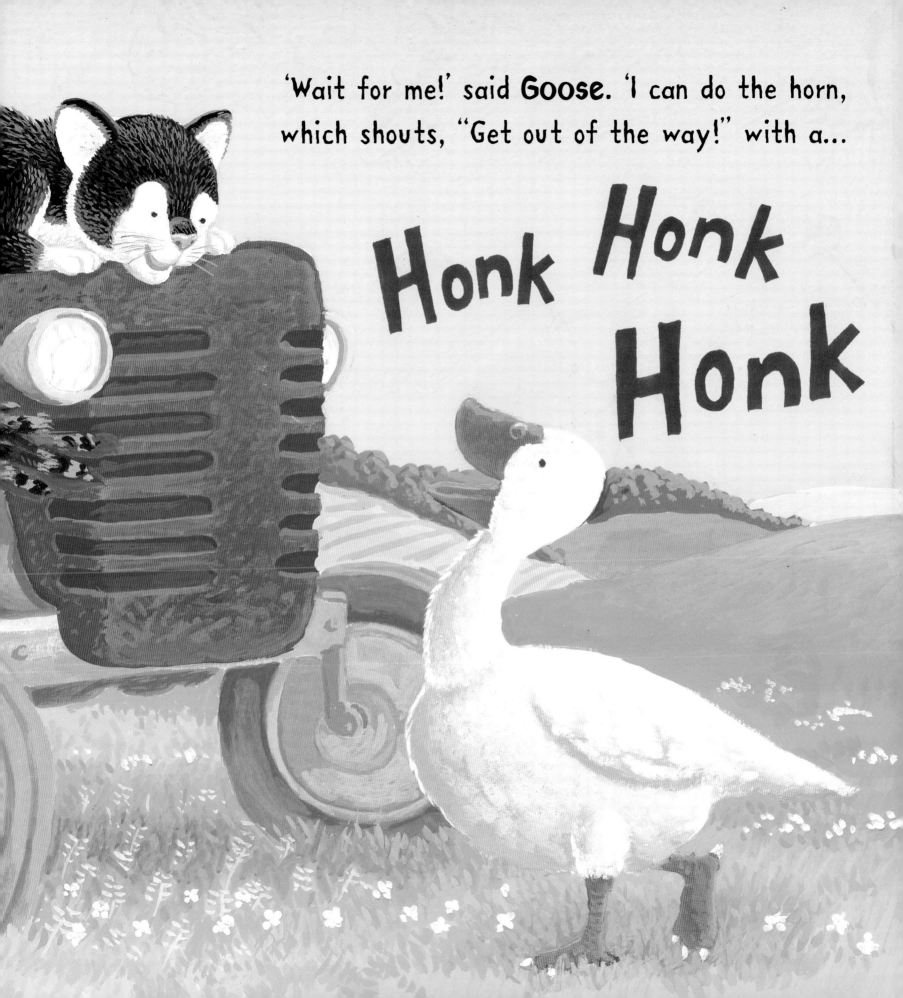

'Wait for me!' said **Goose**. 'I can do the horn, which shouts, "Get out of the way!" with a...

Honk Honk Honk

'I can do the engine when the tractor goes fast,' said **Cow.**
'It gets louder and louder
and sounds like this...

MOOOOOOOO!

'Let's do it again!' said **Cat.**
'We can all join in,' said Mouse.

'But what about Farmer Dougal?' said **Sheep**.

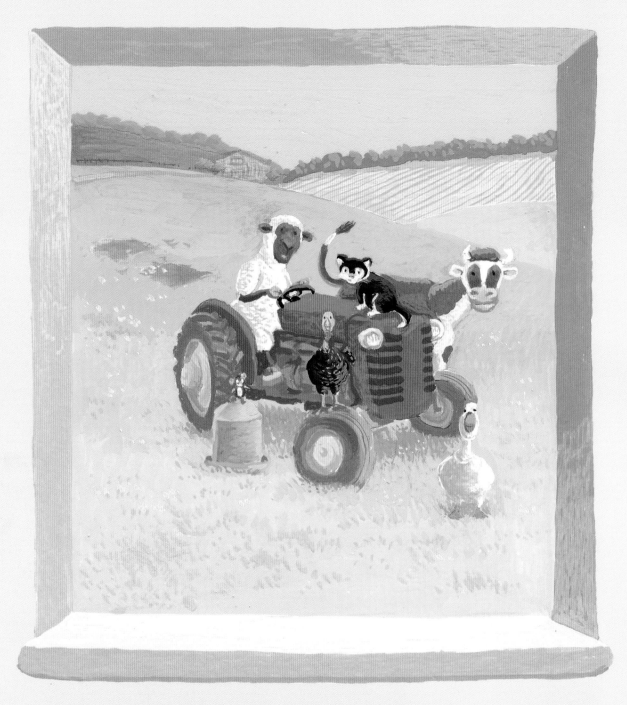

Then **Cat**, **Turkey**, Mouse, **Goose** and **Cow**
looked at **Sheep** with six soppy smiles and said...

# P·L·E·A·S·E

'I'm turning
        the engine on...'

'All right,' said **Sheep**. 'Ready...

'and the tractor is driving off
down the lane...'

GOBBLE GOBBLE
GOBBLE GOBBLE
GOBBLE GOBBLE

The great big wheels
are rolling round and round...'

SQUEAK SQUEAK
SQUEAK

But then...

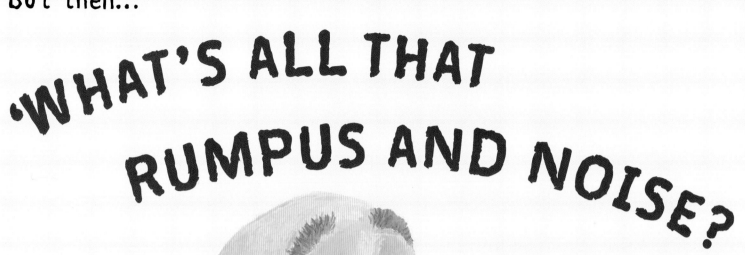

'WHAT'S ALL THAT RUMPUS AND NOISE? IT SOUNDS LIKE

'The horn is saying, "Get out of the way!" with a...'

# Honk Honk Honk

'And the engine is going
faster and faster...'

moooo
ooooo
oooooo
oooo

SOMEONE IS DRIVING OFF WITH MY TRACTOR!'

'QUICK!' cried **Sheep**. 'It's Farmer Dougal...

Farmer Dougal looked out of the window...
and there was his big red tractor, safe and sound.

'I must have been dreaming,' he said.
Then he pulled the curtains shut and climbed
back into bed.

Then **Cow** looked at **Sheep**,

**Turkey** looked at **Sheep**.

Mouse looked at **Sheep**,

Cat looked at **Sheep**,

Goose looked at **Sheep**,

and **Sheep** looked at them all with a big, goofy grin and said...